MW00947995

We dedicate this book to our
children and grandchildren.

www.mascotbooks.com
roselopezbooks.com

When the Day Ends... and Dreams Begin...

For more information, please contact:
Mascot Books
620 Herndon Parkway #320
Herndon, VA 20170
info@mascotbooks.com

Library of Congress Control Number: 2018911602

CPSIA Code: PRT1118A
ISBN-13: 978-1-64307-066-7

Printed in the United States

When the Day Ends...
and
Dreams
Begin...

Don Rose & Javier Lopez

illustrated by Rayanne Vieira

Rocky the Rock, the Rock That Could Walk

Once upon a time, there was a rock named Rocky who lived at the bottom of the ocean. Rocky always wished he could be on land and see the world. He had already seen everything he wanted to see of the ocean, and he was bored. Lucky for him, a storm was brewing right off the coast of California in Carmel Bay.

Rocky saw the winds blowing and the waves crashing, and he hoped and prayed that they would be strong enough to carry him far away. And with a little luck, they did!

"Wow!" said Rocky as he landed on the beach with a *thud*. "So, this is land."

As Rocky dried off in the sun, he watched as the people around him walked up and down the beach, picnicked in the sun, and played in the surf.

And look! A small boy was coming toward him. Rocky tried to look his shiniest. Maybe he'd take Rocky on a picnic!

The boy came closer and closer. Then he outstretched his arm, picked up Rocky, and threw him right back into the ocean!

Ooooh, the little rock was so mad. He rocked back and forth and steamed and shook. He wanted to be back on that beach he had dreamed about for so long. He just had to get back there.

Rocky was so upset, he didn't even notice the two little legs that had just popped out of his body. They were skinny but sure, and Rocky walked right out of the ocean. *Wow!* he thought. *I'm Rocky the Rock and I can walk!*

By the time Rocky made it back to the beach, the sun was setting in a brilliant orange and red. Before long, night would be upon him. Rocky was tired from his long walk on his new legs, so when he found a dry spot, he collapsed and fell sound asleep. The next morning, the warm sun heated Rocky's back.

1

Rocky woke up immediately and looked around. "I'm still on the beach!" he said. "And I still have legs!"

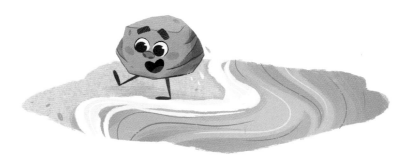

He yelled for all the other rocks to see him, but rocks don't talk or walk, so none of the other rocks even noticed. But it didn't matter; the little rock was still so happy.

As the day wore on, people gathered on the beach to enjoy the day. Soon, Rocky found himself in the middle of a crowd of teenagers. Their music was loud and their food smelled great. Rocky wanted to get closer, so he inched over to a French fry that had fallen on the ground.

Just as he was about there, a girl reached over and set a cold can of Pepsi on his back. *What in the world?* thought Rocky. *This is cold!*

So Rocky used his new legs and carried that Pepsi can right on over to a sunny spot on the beach.

"Hey!" the girl cried. "Who moved my Pepsi?"

Rocky heard everyone laugh as they looked around.

"Look!" Someone pointed to Rocky. "There it is!"

"Did that rock move?" said another boy. "Rocks can't move!"

And that's when Rocky the Rock, the rock that could walk, decided he was going to have a very fun time living on the beach.

The next time you go to the beach in Carmel-by-the-Sea, be careful where you place things. You never know if Rocky the Rock might carry them away.

Two Sides to a Story

A pocketful of sunshine, a little pep in my step,
A smile on my face, the last time I checked.

Off to find a rainbow and that pot full of gold;
There's money to be made, at least that's what I'm told.

I accepted the challenge; I know the obstacles I'll face
So excited I am to find that wonderful place.

Wish me luck on this journey that I'm about to take
And if you're lucky enough, I'll share the money I make.

Okay boys, are you ready for this?
Our pot of gold is on everyone's list.

We better be ready to put up a fight.
Them taking our treasure? Well that isn't right.

Who do they think they are, thinking they can just take
All our hard work in this gold that we make?

Look over yonder, I see someone in view!
Load up the cannon; better yet, load up two!

This is our gold, it belongs to us.
If you come to take it, then fight we must.

3

Uncle Frank

Once upon a time, there was a couple who wanted a dog, but not just any dog. They wanted a silly, loyal, happy dog. A dog that would bring them joy. So, they looked and looked and looked, until they finally found a small, red-haired, silly, and happy dog. His coat was shiny and long, he had intelligent, deep brown eyes, and he was warm and cute. They brought the dog home and gave him a warm, safe bed, cool water, and a wonderful yard to run around.

Now, a dog like this needed a special name. Something unique, something that reminded people that he was a special dog. They thought and thought and thought. Suddenly, they knew! They had found a name that was definitely unique, definitely special, and definitely memorable. *Uncle Frank*.

Everyone loved the name, especially Uncle Frank. He seemed so proud as he strutted around the neighborhood, hearing what people had to say.

"Hi, Uncle Frank!"

"Uncle Frank sure is handsome today!"

Now everyone had an Uncle Frank they could love. The couple would joke with their friends when they went to the grocery store.

"Hey, we need to pick up some dog food for Uncle Frank!"

"What?! That's awful!"

Then they would laugh and laugh because they had a special, silly, loyal and happy dog named Uncle Frank.

Dragonfly

Like most people, I think dragonflies are cool
But a dragon, really, who are they trying to fool?

I see you have wings that help you soar through the sky
But I'm not convinced you're part dragon, sorry, I cannot lie.

I see your long tail behind you, you think that sums it up?
Your tail and wings, well, that's not enough.

You look more like a fly than a ferocious big dragon!
I should have watched what I said; you'll never guess what did happen.

The dragonfly looked at me and then made a weird sound;
He called more dragonflies, and so I hit the ground.

There were so many, more than I could see.
I thought, *This is it, they're going to eat me.*

The sound from their wings was like thunder from the sky.
I started to yell, "STOP! I don't want to die!"

"Silly child," one said, "we mean you no harm,
We've just come to show you our wonderful charm."

They flew around me so fast I started to pant.
Next thing I knew, I was as small as an ant.

When I looked up and saw them, they were huge as could be,
Then the one that had spoken landed right next to me.

"Hop on young child. Let's go for a ride."
We rode up and down and flew side to side.

We soared over water and I felt so refreshed,
Then he flew up so high, I nearly lost my breath!

The free fall back down, my gosh, that was the best,
But I asked to land because I needed some rest.

I'm sorry dragonfly, but now I know
You might not be as big as a dragon, but you do have their soul.

Not only that, but you have magic as well.
Dragonflies are part dragon, that's the truth I will tell.

Amazing Me

Has anyone ever told you how great you are?
How you shine so bright like the brightest star?

You're so unique, there are none like you.
So, with all this greatness, what will you do?

As for me, I let my imagination soar.
Every day is an adventure, a new world to explore!

One day I'm an astronaut, deep in outer space,
Searching for new worlds to discover a new place.

Or a race car driver, who drives real fast,
Trying to reach first place and avoid being last!

But if I end up in last place, I'm not bothered the least.
I'm glad I still tried and drove like a beast.

Some days I'm a construction worker building a new home.
The last one I built was the shape of a dome.

So much to do, so much to choose,
With all of these choices, you know we can't lose!

How about a doctor who helps with a pet?
(I believe that kind of a doctor is called a vet.)

That would be fun, so many animals we'd see!
A dog or a horse—how happy we'd be!

How about a people doctor, who helps kids like me?
Helps fix them up so they can run free.

Or a marathon runner, cross-country, or track,
Just keep on moving, don't stay where you're at!

The sky is the limit, so reach for the stars.
The future is bright and the future is ours!

So, if no one has ever told you how great you could be,
Just shout to the world, "I'm an Amazing Me!"

The Ocean

I love you, Ocean, and the sound that you make.
When you crash on the shore, my breath you do take.

How you reflect the beauty of the bright blue sky
As dolphins and whales together swim by.

As you dance with the surfers, you all become one,
And when dusk begins to settle you tuck away our sun.

I love when you draw back, when the tide deems it low,
And a glimpse of the wonders inside you does show.

Crabs running amuck as starfish just rest,
Time spent with you is truly the best.

So, for now, dear Ocean, I bid you good day,
'Till next time my friend, again we shall play.

The Little Puddle

Once upon a time, there was a depression in a big asphalt parking lot next to a creek. *Oh boy! I'm a puddle*, thought the depression.

Soon it rained and the little puddle felt important. Kids would walk through it wearing raincoats and big rubber boots, splashing and stomping joyously in the water. The puddle loved the attention, but when the hot sun came out, the puddle dried up.

"Heck, I'm a nobody now," said the puddle sadly. Summer came and the dried-up puddle was all alone. No one came to play.

Before long, the rains came back and the puddle felt happy and important again! Ducks would stop by for a day of swimming and rest. A big frog came to visit one day. The puddle was thrilled.

This is great! the puddle thought. *If only I could find a way to keep this water during the summer, then I just know I'll stay important!*

That summer the puddle dried up again, but one day the water in the nearby creek suddenly jumped over its banks and filled up the puddle!

Great! thought the puddle. *I'm back in action!* Birds stopped in, a cat drank from the edges, and a small plant began to grow. The puddle was so happy to be important again.

One day, there was a big fire in the building pretty close to the puddle. The firemen came with their big red trucks and got right to work trying to put out the fire. Before long, they used up all the water from their trucks, but the fire was not out! They threw their hoses in the creek and kept fighting. They dried up the creek, and the fire still wasn't out!

"What are we going to do? The fire is almost out, but we've run out of water!" cried a fireman.

"Hey look, there's a puddle! Maybe that will finish the job!" said another. They put their hoses in the puddle and it worked! The fire was out! The puddle felt so proud.

"Hey, this puddle helped us put out the fire," said the fire chief. "Let's build it up so it can have water all year round."

The little puddle beamed.

So now any time you see a puddle, think of it as the puddle that put out a fire and give it a hearty wave.

Loose Teeth

My parents want to pull my loose teeth, but I said, "No way!
Give them some time—they'll fall out one day."

They offered me gifts and even money, so I had to think twice.
A miniature pony would really be nice.

A trip to the theme park with unlimited rides,
Or how about the water park with unlimited slides?

"You can go to both," they said, "just let us give those teeth a tug.
Be brave, Buttercup. It's in there quite snug!"

"We don't want to hurt you or cause you any grief."
"Oh really? Are you guys just collectors of teeth?

That's the tooth fairy's job and I don't think she quit.
My teeth need to stay right where they sit."

"But kiddo, the dentist said they need to come out."
"Well, that dentist didn't know what he's talking about!"

"But you can get money from us and the tooth fairy too.
Is there anything we can say to help convince you?"

"Sorry folks, I suggest you just quit.
The pulling of my teeth, I am not having it!"

That was the end of that, and I
        went straight to sleep.
When I awoke the next morning,
        I had swallowed those teeth.

If I would have listened,
        a gift I would have got.
But due to my stubbornness,
        I didn't get squat!

Off to the Races

Off to the races, today I will go.
Can't wait for the turtles to put on a good show.

I know what you're thinking: a turtle race?
Who'd want to watch turtles move at such a slow pace?

These aren't the type of turtles that you've seen, my friend,
Those laws of nature, you know, those laws, they do bend.

You don't believe the things that I have spoke?
Then come with me and witness that it's no joke!

We have to go through the forest and find the secret spot.
You have to be invited, or else welcomed you are not.

But since you're with me, they will let you in.
Are you ready to go and watch the fun begin?

Off to the races we go, so much fun you'll find!
All the things you'll see will tickle your mind.

We finally made it, it's about to begin!
Let me do the talking, so we can get in.

That was a close one, because they've never seen you before.
For a second, I thought we weren't gonna get through the door!

So here we are at the great turtle races!
I love this place and all the happy faces.

The first race coming up is when they ride on a fox—
Told you they were different, so think outside the box!

Bet you'd never thought you would see things like this!
Keep your eyes on the track so the race you won't miss.

Next one coming up is the eagle race.
I see the excitement all over your face!

Look how fast they go and how high they soar!
But this isn't it, don't worry, there's more.

Like when they roll down a hill while inside a tire.
If you didn't see it for yourself, you would've called me a liar.

Then there's the mole race, where they head underground.
Sometimes they fall off and scream to be found.

Last but not least is the homemade rocket.
Sometimes, these turtles don't know how to stop it.

It's a dangerous race, so different measures they take;
That's why they race over the wonderful lake.

If things go wrong they just make a splash—
Jump in the water and let their rocket crash.

So, there you have it, you've seen it for yourself.
Watching these races is good for your health!

Thanks for joining me, I hope to see you again
At these awesome races. Till next time, my friend!

Tuna Noodle Casserole and Caramel Cake

Once upon a time, there was a girl named Gigi who just loved to spend time with her grandparents, especially her Grammy. One day, when her parents left for four days to celebrate their anniversary, Gigi asked her Grammy to teach her how to cook.

"Sure!" said Grammy. "Let's make a Tuna Noodle Casserole and Caramel Cake."

"Grammy, why do you call it a 'Tuna Noodle Casserole and Caramel Cake'?"

"A fun name makes it taste better, that's why!" said Grammy.

So, Grammy and Gigi went to the store and bought all of the ingredients. On the way home, they stopped for some tasty frozen yogurt from Menchies.

"*Yummmm!*" said Gigi and Grammy.

When they got home, Grammy got a stool for Gigi and a pretty apron.

"Now stir the noodles, and then we'll make some sauce for our Tuna Noodle Casserole and Caramel Cake," said Grammy.

When the cooking was done, they ate the great meal together. Gigi couldn't wait to tell her parents that she and Grammy had made a delicious Tuna Noodle Casserole and Caramel Cake.

Halloween

Zombies, goblins, witches, and stew.
Princesses, soldiers, and ghosts that go "Boo!"

Candy and treats and people to trick,
Houses so scary, I think I will skip.

But not too many, because candy I need.
Breakfast, lunch, and dinner on candy I'll feed!

When it's all said and done, the dentist I'll see
To pick up new teeth made just for me.

The Beautiful Silver Fish

Once upon a time, there was a family who lived by the shore. The dad would hold his breath and dive into the water every day to catch fish to sell at the market so he could support his wife and four children. Some days when he didn't catch any fish, the family was very poor.

One day, the dad spotted a beautiful silver fish swimming through the water. *If only I could catch that fish and sell it at the market*, he thought. *Then I may have enough money to get the kids new shoes.*

But he could not catch the silver fish that day. It was quick and swam right away from him. Every day afterwards, he looked for that beautiful silver fish with hopes he could capture it.

One day, he spotted the beautiful silver fish again swimming lazily in the water. But when the fish saw him, he swam deep into the ocean, into a dark cave near the bottom of the ocean.

But the man was a great swimmer, so he followed. When he made it to the cave, he tried to peek in, but it was too dark. He took out his small waterproof flashlight and tried again to peek into the cave.

There were shiny green, gold, and red eyes looking back at him! The man got scared and quickly swam back to the surface. What was in that cave?

When he got home, he told his wife about the silver fish and how he thought it would help his family. Then he told her about the cave full of different colored eyes that he followed the fish into.

He was afraid to go in after the silver fish.

"Why don't you take your waterproof camera on your next dive and take a picture of that cave?" his wife suggested. "Then we can find out what's in the cave without having to go in."

"Good idea," said the man.

The next day, the man took his camera with him on his dive. He saw the silver fish again and chased it, and it once more swam into the dark cave. The man took out his camera, took a picture, then swam away. He took the film to a shop in the town so he could see the picture. When he went to pick up the picture, the shopkeeper asked where the photo had been taken. The man wouldn't tell.

The man took the picture home to his wife and they looked at it together. The cave was still dark and deep, but they looked as hard as they could until they could just barely make out the glittering green, gold, and red at the back of the cave with the silver fish. Then the man got excited, and his wife smiled. They knew what to do next.

Early the next day, the man swam to the cave without looking for the silver fish. He swam confidently into the cave, and found that the gold was actual gold, the green was emeralds, and the red was rubies. He was so happy! He grabbed a handful of jewels and swam away.

With the treasure, he bought a nice home for his family, new clothes, and good food. He would go back to the cave every so often, but only to get as many jewels as he needed to keep his family safe and happy. Now and then he would see the silver fish, and when he did, he'd give it a wave and a wink.

Waves

Waves are glorious as they come crashing down.
The bigger they are, the louder the sound.

But even the small ones are soothing to see.
Right by those waves is where I want to be.

Sitting on the beach or posted in a stance,
Those wonderful waves put me in a trance.

Is it strictly white water or will a barrel form?
Watching waves take shape is like watching them be born.

I see the people playing in the water, having so much fun,
And when the waves come crashing down, the kids start to run.

Or the surfers on their boards, waiting for that chance
To meet with a wave and get caught up in the dance.

The wave is the lead, and the surfer just follows.
If the surfer's not careful, he'll surely get swallowed!

No bad intentions the wave has been given.
To be able to ride it, for that surfer is living.

Even from a distance, to hear them is profound,
Those beautiful waves crashing onto the ground.

The Ants on the Hill

Those ants on the hill, what a wonderful sight!
Marching and working from day until night.

Lines so straight, distracted they're not.
On the path they're heading. You don't want to get caught!

If you do, well, I wish you the best
They'll pick you right up and carry you with the rest,

The rest of the food they have, or just the debris.
To tell you the truth, better you than me!

They don't mean you harm, they just don't want to stop.
Getting the job done, to them, means a whole lot.

So, if you see those ants marching on by,
Step to the side and wave hello and goodbye.

The Little Duck Who Wanted to be Taller

Once upon a time, a baby duck was born into a duck family. The dad and mom duck and brothers and sisters were so excited to have a little duck around. The problem was that the little duck was always struggling to keep up. When they went for a walk, the little duck would be running at the back of the line just trying to stay with his family.

"Oooh, I wish I had bigger feet to keep up!" he panted.

When the family stopped to eat the berries off a plant, the little duck could only get the berries at the very bottom of the plant or the ones his family dropped.

"Oooh, I wish I were taller!"

When they swam in the pond, he paddled like crazy to keep up.

"Oooh, I wish I had longer legs!"

One day when they were walking in the woods, a big net fell over the whole family and they were trapped.

"Oh no!" cried the family "What shall we do?"

The dad and mom duck were so worried. The brother ducks said, "Don't worry, we'll break the net." But they were not strong enough.

The sister ducks said, "Don't worry, we'll peck at the ropes and break them." But they couldn't.

The little duck walked in and out of the trap saying, "What shall we do? What shall we do?"

The whole family stopped and watched the little duck freely walking in and out.

"Little duck!" they all shouted. "You're small and can get out of the trap. Go out and pull the rope and let us all out."

The little duck tried and tried but the net was too heavy. He walked into the forest and saw a big strong lion sleeping. "Hey lion!" he yelled. But the lion just slept. He went to the back of the lion and kicked him as hard as he could.

The lion jumped up looking for an enemy, but only saw the little duck. "What do you want, little duck?"

The duck said, "I'm little and can't pull the net off my family, will you help?"

"Sure," said the lion.

The big strong lion pulled the net off the duck family and they all were free. The little duck saved his family, and they were all proud of him and loved him. The little duck was proud too.

The Winner

I picked a winner I couldn't believe.
I dug so deep, but it didn't even bleed.

People were looking, guess they wanted to watch.
It was slimy and green, a real top notch.

The best part of all, you should have seen their face
When I stuck out my tongue and went in for a taste!

A Pirate's Life

Shiver me timbers, you scurvy dogs.
May you walk the plank and hop off like frogs!

Oh, to be a pirate with a parrot named Pat,
With a patch on my eye and a feather in my hat.

With a ship all my own, and my own crew,
A pirate's life for me, oh, the things I would do.

I would sail the seas in search of new lands,
Eat what I want without washing my hands.

Skip taking showers, I'll just jump in the sea,
Yell, "Ahoy me mateys! A pirate's life for me!"

Dig up buried treasure and then bury it again.
Battle other ships because my treasure I defend.

There would be no school, just an occasional class
Of swashbuckling, sword fighting, and talking pirate trash.

Maybe arts and crafts to make a cool flag.
How 'bout learning to sew your own treasure bag?

To hold rubies and diamonds, whatever we take
With pictures of skulls and a poisonous snake?

Enough with the classes,
     the rest we'd learn on the sea,
Oh yes, me mateys, a pirate's life for me.

PIRATES RULE

A Fish Named George

Once upon a time, there was a happy, handsome fish named George. He swam the warm waters and was a friendly fish. He had only one problem, though. He would have fun with the other fish right up until the time they would ask him his name.

"George?" They would shout and laugh. "That's a terrible name!" They swam away laughing.

George laughed too, kind of, and swam away.

He met a big whale and asked, "What's your name?"

The whale said proudly, "My name is Wally the Whale, what's your name?"

"My name is George."

Wally the Whale laughed and swam away saying, "That's a terrible name!"

George swam on.

He met a swordfish and said, "What's your name?"

"I'm Sammy the Swordfish," said the swordfish. "What's your name?"

"I'm George."

Sammy the Swordfish just laughed and swam away. "George is a terrible name!"

Poor old George felt terrible. Soon he saw a pretty girl fish and began to talk to her. Soon she said, "What's your name?"

He looked down and said, "I don't want to tell you because everyone makes fun of my name and leaves. What's your name?"

"My name is Georgia," said the girl fish proudly.

"MY NAME IS GEORGE!" said George, now proud and happy.

George and Georgia were married and had a big family, all named George and Georgia.

This Old Bike

It's been an adventure, bike, this journey we've shared.
I remember our first ride, boy was I scared!

How your front wheel wobbled and I'd lose all control,
Like that one time we both crashed right into a pole.

Not just one time, it was more than a few.
How about launching off curbs, and all the tricks we would do?

Remember those dogs that chased us and I'd peddle real fast,
And the neighbor who got mad because we rode on his grass?

They never did catch us, those mangy old mutts.
When we were together I always had guts.

No road was too rugged, no hill was too steep.
I always enjoyed it when we'd launch over a creek.

Sadly, I've outgrown you, so our time together is now done.
I love you, old bike, thank you for all the fun.

My Brother

My brother is wild. No really, he is.
Everything he touches he thinks is his!

If you knock on our door and he opens it up,
Well, all I can say is you better just duck.

Be quick on your toes and move really fast.
The last person who didn't is now in a cast.

He's a wild creature I once tried to return.
My parents weren't happy, a lesson I learned.

He got me back once I fell asleep
By shoving his dirty diaper inside my sheet.

I woke up the next morning to a horrible smell.
You know what it was, I don't have to tell.

The stork must have left him here by mistake.
If he comes back to get him, that would be great.

As a matter of fact, I'll write him a letter,
But mom keeps saying that things will get better.

Tell that to my doll who has a missing head,
And my coloring books he decided to shred!

When I think that's it, I can't take it anymore,
He does something funny and I fall to the floor.

I start laughing so hard I can't seem to stop—
Now that I think about it, he does that a lot.

He gives me hugs when I'm sad and kisses my face.
You know what, I'm glad he got left at our place!

He may drive me nuts, but I love that twerp,
So I give him a hug, and he pees on my skirt!

Mommmmmmm!!!!

I'm a Frog, I Just Love Being a Frog

Once upon a time, a little frog left his pond to visit his grandmother in the big pond beyond the hills. The little frog was happy and excited for this big adventure as he hopped away.

Soon, he ran into a mouse. "Hi, I'm a frog," he said proudly. "I'm a mouse," said the mouse.

"What can you do?" said the frog. "I can hop and make this great sound: *RrrrBbbbTttt!*"

"Gee, I can't do that," said the mouse.

"Too bad," said the frog proudly and hopped on. "I just love being a frog."

Soon, he ran into a lion. "What the heck are you?" said the little frog, "You're so big."

"I'm a lion," said the lion.

"What can you do?" asked the frog. "I can hop and jump and make this great sound: *RrrrBbbbTttt!*"

"Gee," said the lion, "I can't do any of those things."

"That's too bad," said the frog. "You are so big. I just love being a frog."

Soon, he ran into an eagle. "Whoa, what the heck are you?" said the little frog.

"I," said the eagle, "am the great eagle."

"I can hop and jump and make this great sound: *RrrrBbbbTttt!*" said the frog.

"Wow," said the eagle. "I can't do that, but I can fly."

"What's 'fly'?" said the frog.

"I'll show you," said the eagle.

He took the little frog and flew up into the sky. "Whoo!" said the frog. "Doesn't this scare you?"

"Nope," said the eagle.

"Hey, I can see my grandmother's pond from up here," said the frog. "Put me down."

The eagle gently put the frog on the ground. The frog said, "That was so fun, but I just love being a frog."

And the little frog hopped into the big pond to see his grandmother. He told her all about his adventures and they both laughed and said, "We just love being frogs!"

The Girl with the Crazy, Curly, Wild Hair

Once upon a time, there was a little girl named Cora who was a blue-eyed girl with crazy, curly, wild hair. Her hair went this way and that way, and that way and this way. She laughed and smiled and her silly hair flew this way and that way. You could brush it, you could wet it, you could try and tame it, but her crazy, curly, wild hair just sprung out as quickly as it could. Everyone just loved her crazy, curly, wild hair.

Cora just loved her hair and would shake her head just to see what the new look would be. Wherever she went, people would comment on her hair. Her biggest hair fan was her Papa Baj.

He just loved, loved, loved her crazy, curly, wild hair. She always laughed when she saw her Papa Baj take the ten hairs he had left on his head and tried to make them look wild.

"Sorry Papa Baj, you lose."

Papa Baj just laughed. He wanted crazy, curly, wild hair, but Cora was the owner of the craziest, curliest, and wildest hair. She would always smile when she saw herself in the mirror and think, "I'm different and I love it."

Sea Star

Once upon a time, there was a tall, beautiful ship that sailed the seas. It was a big, strong ship named the Sea Star. The ship loved her name and carrying the passengers all over the seven seas. When she took her passengers to the hot Caribbean islands, she kept everyone cool inside. When she traveled to cold Alaska, she kept everyone warm.

The Sea Star just loved being a big strong passenger ship, and always honked her mighty horn when she met all the smaller boats around the world. She especially loved to go through the narrow Panama Canal where all the people marveled at her size and sparkle.

Honk! Honk! "Hi boats, hi birds and fish, hi people!"

Even when the open oceans rocked the Sea Star back and forth, she still loved sailing them. No matter how hard the ocean tried to sway her off course, the Sea Star stayed strong, sturdy, and steady. She had a mission—to show her passengers the big, beautiful world—and nothing could stop her from completing it!

A Reindeer Named Winter

Isn't it amazing some things that happen in life,
Sometimes they're strange and aren't always right.

I'll tell you this story that I still can't believe.
The truth of the matter, it happened to me.

Well I was a part of it, but more so my daughter,
But I'll share the story. Why not? I'm her father.

It started one time when the weather was cold.
She wanted another pet, but I wasn't quite sold.

We already had a dog, a turtle, and we used to have a snake,
But we let him go because the cage he did hate.

I said, "We're good, two pets are enough."
Ooh, my daughter's sad face made it quite rough!

Yet she was determined, so a wish she had made,
And I thought in due time her desire would fade.

But that bright ol' star heard her loud and clear!
Who would have ever imagined that wish would appear?

The next morning at breakfast, she was as happy as can be.
She was all giggles and laughter, no longer upset with me.

"What's so funny?" I asked with a smile on my face.
"Oh nothing, Dad, I just love this place."

So, I finished eating and to my backyard I went,
And I noticed my favorite tree's branches were twisted and bent.

What could have happened to cause all this mess?
Then I noticed my bushes had become a lot less.

I walked around the yard to see what else I could find.
Maybe my fence was broken, but no, that was fine.

I heard a noise and felt some movement of sorts,
Like hooves on the ground and animal snorts.

I turned real quick but nothing was there,
But all over my clothes I had animal hair!

All of a sudden, I heard a noise on my roof.
The sound of an animal stomping its hoof.

No way, I thought, so I grabbed a ladder quick.
As I was climbing up, I started to slip!

I closed my eyes and began to fall,
But I didn't hit the floor, not even the wall.

I was just floating, suspended in air.
I couldn't open my eyes, because I was so scared.

But I had to be brave, I had to look,
And what I saw had me quite shook!

The reason I was okay, well you wouldn't believe!
In a reindeer's mouth was my sweater's sleeve!

I yelled for my wife and outside she ran.
It was the highest pitched scream she had heard from a man.

She turned the corner and then she just froze,
Whispered real softly, "A reindeer's eating your clothes."

Then out came my daughter who said, "I'm so glad you've met!
Dad, this is Winter, my lovely new pet."

I looked up at Winter; she was as sweet as can be.
How could I say no to a pet who just saved me?

Then my wife set up the ladder and down I came.
I knew our lives would no longer be the same.

A reindeer? I thought. There's no forest nearby.
But a shiny tag around her neck caught my eye.

When I tried to look, my hand she would lick,
But I finally read what it said, "Property of Nick."

It couldn't be, I thought. What shall I do?
Well, that's another story I'll have to share with you.

Shark

"Hello shark, lion of the sea,
King of the ocean with all of those teeth.

My name is Johnny, how do you do?
There are so many questions I'd like to ask you!

Are you really that angry and mean all the time?
Do you eat what you want, whatever you find?

Why are you always swimming alone?
Where do you live? Where is your home?"

"Well, my home is anywhere I want it to be
In this glorious and wonderful, beautiful sea.

I'm not alone, just look on my back.
I have a friend with me wherever I'm at.

He helps keep me clean, he is my best mate.
Look how clean I am! Don't I look great?

As for my eating, it's whatever I choose,
And as for those people who were bitten, well, I got confused.

When I'm swimming in the ocean, so deep below,
People look like seals beneath the sun's glow.

Truth of the matter is, people taste quite gross,
But seals and fish, I love them the most!

Attack them on purpose, never would I.
Accidents happen and avoid them I try.

Please let them know how sorry I am,
And why they're afraid of me, I do understand.

As for being mean, I'm not in the least!
I'm not a bloodthirsty savage beast.

I'm just a shark who is living his life
In this enormous ocean and its radiant sights.

So, did I answer your questions, what you wanted to know?"
"Yes, Mr. Shark, now I'm ready to go."

"Okay Johnny, I'm glad I could help you understand.
Now grab hold of my fin and I'll take you to land.

Here we are Johnny, the ride's come to an end.
I'm so glad I met you and made a new friend!

Please let the humans know what you have learned."
"I will Mr. Shark, and one day I'll return."

"I look forward to it Johnny, you take care, mate.
Now hurry yourself home before it gets late."

The Little Island

Once upon a time, there was a little island in the Caribbean Sea that was surrounded by a beautiful white sand beach. It had two tall palm trees with a hammock between them. What a wonderful island in the warm sea! The sun rose from the sea in the east and warmed the little island.

"Hi, Sun," the Island said. "How are you today?"

"Hi, Island," said the Sun. "Today is going to be nice and warm with a light tropical breeze."

"Oh good," said the little island. "I hope someone comes to visit me today, to play on my white beaches, sit on my island grasses, and lay in my special hammock in the warm breeze."

Soon a boat appeared, and the young captain Brett said, "Here's a wonderful spot to stop and enjoy the day." Captain Brett and his crewmate, Jeremiah, jumped ashore and laughed and played on the happy island in the Caribbean Sea. Captain Brett lay on the hammock and rocked back and forth in the light, warm breeze. Jeremiah played in the sand and wiggled his toes in the warm water. They loved the little island, and the little island loved them too.

"This is our island," they claimed and they laughed. "It's our paradise!"

Soon, the boys and their little boat left, promising to return. Then the sun set in the west with a big beautiful sky of red and orange. "See you tomorrow, bright and early, Sun," said the little island.

"See you soon!" said the Sun.

The Little Girl Who Couldn't Wait...Until She Could

Once upon a time there was a little girl named Elizabeth, but everyone called her E. E just couldn't wait for school to be over and summer vacation to begin. "Hurry, hurry, hurry!" she said every day after school.

Then one day, school was over for the year. E was going to spend the summer with her grandparents at Lake Tahoe. Now, Lake Tahoe had lots of things to do. Boating, swimming, parasailing, hiking, horseback riding, lying on the beach, peewee golf, and lots more.

"We'll have to pack before going to Lake Tahoe," said her mom.

E couldn't wait to pack. "Hurry, hurry, hurry!" she said as she threw her clothes in her suitcase.

Before long, it was time to leave. "Now we'll have to drive to the airport so we can get on the airplane to Grandpa and Grammy's," said her mom.

"Hurry, hurry, hurry!" she said, throwing her suitcase in the car.

When they arrived at the airport, E was ready to go. "Hurry, hurry, hurry!" she said to the plane. Then the plane was in the air.

"We'll be at our destination in three hours," said the pilot.

"Hurry, hurry, hurry!" she said.

Then the plane landed. She saw her grandparents. Big hugs, big kisses, oh what fun!

"Okay," said Grandpa, "Two hours in the car, then we'll be at Lake Tahoe for the summer."

"Oh good, oh good, oh good!" said the little girl, E.

As the miles went by, the little girl said, "Hurry, hurry, hurry!"

Then they were there. They went into the house, got settled, then went out to the beach. Her mom said, "We'll spend the summer here, then go back home and back to school."

"Go slow, go slow, go slow," said E, smiling.

The Cloud

I'm just a cloud floating through the sky,
I take different shapes to catch your eye.

It's my pleasure in making all of you guess.
What shape did I form, can you pass the test?

Am I a dog in the park that's chasing a ball,
Or kids in school running down the hall?

I love watching you sitting there watching me,
Guessing these amazing shapes that I love to be.

That's not all I do, I give you some shade
When you're playing in the park or watching a parade.

When you ride your bike or swim in a pool,
I block the sun to help keep you cool.

The best of all is the rain that I bring.
They made a movie of it where people dance and sing.

It brings life to the fields, the plants, and the trees,
It makes puddles so deep that they reach your knees!

I love watching you splash and jump around,
Enjoying all the water that has covered the ground.

It's always a pleasure to watch you from so high,
But I have to leave now, so enjoy the blue sky.

The Little Girl Who Was Inappropriate

Once upon a time, there was a fun, lively, happy, full-of-life little girl who just loved life. She loved everyone and everyone loved her. Her smile made you smile, her talkative nature made you want to talk, and her fun laugh made you want to laugh.

She loved school because of all the friends she made and all the interesting things she learned, but she did not like her Spanish class. She loved the Spanish food, but she just didn't want to take the time to learn the language.

One day, her parents got a call from school to discuss her "inappropriate behavior." Her dad was concerned, her mom was worried. When they sat down, the school counselor said, "Your little girl has been inappropriate."

"What did she do?" asked the dad.

"What could she have done?" wondered the mom.

"Well," said the counselor, "in Spanish class, sometimes she opens the window of the class and yells out 'Help me, someone! I'm so bored with Spanish! Help!' and the whole class laughs and laughs and giggles and it takes a while to get everyone settled again."

"Well," said the dad.

"Okay," said the mom. "We will talk to her."

That night at dinner, her mom and dad said, "We talked to your counselor at school today about something that you do at school that is considered inappropriate."

"What is it?" said the little girl.

Her mom and dad looked at each other. Then her dad said, "They told us you open the window and yell out that Spanish is boring."

"Hahaha," laughed the little girl. "I do! Spanish is boring! Everyone feels the same thing—only I say it!"

"You might think it's *abburido*," said her dad.

"But some *estudiantes* may not," said her mom.

"Wow!" said the little girl. "I didn't know you both spoke Spanish!"

"We paid attention in class!" said her dad.

"And you should too!" said her mom.

Mr. Turtle

Mr. Turtle lived in a creek
And was always kind to whomever he'd meet.

He'd swim through the water at a slow pace,
Enjoying every minute of that beautiful place.

There were times he would swim as fast as he could,
And to all the other animals, he looked quite good.

Like the birds in the sky, who thought he'd make a scrumptious lunch.
They snap their beaks and think, munch, munch, munch…

How about those bandits with their masks on their faces?
You know, the raccoons that sneak around these places.

Then there are those creatures who walk on two feet
And catch fish in these waters and throw rocks in the creek.

So much danger, but Mr. Turtle couldn't care less,
All he could think was, *My life is the best!*

I go where I want and have so much to eat,
And so many choices of places to sleep.

So, Mr. Turtle was content as a turtle could be,
Floating down the creek feeling so carefree.

One day while he was floating, he felt a drop hit his face.
The clouds had brought rain to this wonderful place.

He said, "How lovely, more water for me."
So, he swam and he danced while others hid in a tree.

But with all the rain that was dropping, the waters grew rough.
Mr. Turtle said to himself, "Well, enough is enough."

He tried to swim to the creek's bank,
But the harder he tried, the deeper he sank.

When he reached the top of the water, all he could see
Were rapids upon rapids and all kinds of debris.

So, in went his legs, and his head he did tuck.
All he was thinking was, *I hope I have luck!*

He went up and down, round and round,
To the top of the water, and beneath the ground.

All the animals watched as he was tossed to and fro.
They wondered when he'd stop and where he would go.

But if you looked closely while he rushed at a fast pace,
The biggest smile you'd ever see was on Mr. Turtle's face!

He was having a blast in
those waters that rushed,
Riding those waves,
and those waves he did crush!

As the waters settled and drew to a calm,
So far from his home Mr. Turtle had gone.

But in a new place there
are new adventures to seek,
With new explorations
and new friends to meet.

The Guppy That Wanted To Be a Shark

There was a guppy named Pip that wanted to be a shark.
He thought of many scenarios, but didn't know where to start.

"I have to leave my family and be on my own,
Sharks don't swim in schools, they swim all alone.

I'll be brave and strong, swimming so steady,
But leave my family? I don't think I'm ready.

I can still be a shark, but maybe not a great white.
That's okay with me, I'll choose a different type!

How about a hammerhead? They're as tough as can be,
But a hammer for a head? Well, that's not for me.

How about a blue shark? I'm the same color, you see.
That doesn't sound fun, it's just a bigger me!

There's always the whale shark, so massive and huge,
But they're too big and so slow when they move.

Better yet, I'm happy with just being me.
I will stay Pip the guppy and explore all the sea!"

This is Me

Hocus pocus with whoopity-doo,
You better be careful or I'll put a spell on you!

Rattlesnake tails and crocodile tears,
Lizard's snot and cockroach ears.

A pot full of onions mixed with hair gel,
Along with some dirt—what a wonderful smell!

A sorcerer's delight, the concoctions I make,
So real they are, but Mom calls them fake.

Whatever, Mom, don't throw me off track!
All I need is a robe and a wizard's hat.

Mom is upset because a princess I'm not.
I'm working on a potion to get rid of that thought.

Who wants a Prince Charming to give you a kiss?
"Yuck," I say, "Not on my list."

I've always been a sorcerer. Well, I wasn't last week.
I was a Marine in war with foes to defeat.

A week before that you'd catch me jumping off shelves,
A samurai I was who fought wicked elves!

Who knows how long a sorcerer I'll be,
But a princess? Never, that's not for me!

Bob

Once upon a time, there was a little boy who lived in a small town whose name was Roberto. Now, Roberto loved his family and he just loved his name. His mom called him Roberto, his dad called him Roberto, and his sister called him Roberto.

One day his father came home from work and said, "I have wonderful news. We are being transferred to America."

So, they moved to an American city where the family went about meeting new people. This was a very exciting time.

Roberto went to school and met many young boys his age. Roberto was very happy. "What is your name?" Roberto would ask them all.

One boy said, "My name is Jon."

Another said, "My name is Joe."

Another said, "My name is Dan."

What strange names, thought Roberto.

"What is your name?" the boys asked.

"Roberto is my name."

"What a great name," said all the boys. "I wish my name was longer and sounded strong like yours."

"But they are," said Roberto, "my name could be Bob in America, but I like Roberto. Your name, Jon, is Jonathan. Joe is Joseph, and Dan is Daniel."

"Wow," said the boys, "I like that."

So, from then on, the boys used their longer names, and all sounded important!

Key West

Once upon a time, there was a boy who grew up in Key West, a small beautiful island in the Florida Keys. There, he grew up with clear skies and clear turquoise waters filled with multicolored fish. Restaurants had names like Blue Heaven, Green Parrot, and Kermit's. Key lime pie was everywhere and tasted delicious. Colorful chickens and roosters roamed free in Key West and cats were plentiful at the old Hemmingway house in town.

But the boy wondered what lay beyond his small island. So, he made plans to go to another island in New York called Manhattan. When he got there, he was perplexed.

Where was the clear sky? Here there were buildings that rose up to the sky and made the sky small.

Where were the warm turquoise waters? Here, the water was grey and cold and no one snorkeled to see the colorful fish because there were none.

There were too many restaurants, too many people, and no wild chickens and roosters roaming around. There wasn't even any Key lime pie.

New York was different, but it had some fun parts. It was busy, bustling, and full of people, cars, noise, and character. The boy had a good time exploring all of its sights and sounds.

Before long, the boy returned from his adventures to his small, quiet island with clear skies and warm turquoise waters, colorful fish and Key lime pie. It was good to be home.

Lessons on Life

What if in school they taught you about life,
Like things you may face that would test all your might?

Not just science, math, verbs, or past tense,
But how to think logically and use common sense.

To say "thank you" and "you're welcome," "no sir" and "yes ma'am,"
Hold the door for a stranger, or how to shake someone's hand.

How to carry a conversation and look someone in the eye,
Not to give up right away, but continue to try.

To break away from it all, unlike a sheep,
To live life wide awake, and not walk in your sleep.

To not be arrogant or look down on another,
To treat other men and women as sisters and brothers.

It's okay if you're not liked by everyone you meet,
And if you fail at one thing, it doesn't mean defeat.

It could just be a challenge to try that much more,
And not feel weak if that becomes a closed door.

If you fall on your face, go ahead and shake off the dust.
Know not every person you meet deserves your full trust.

There are some deceptive people, selfish as can be,
Who will take what they can from you and from me.

Imagine if this subject schools started to teach,
But the powers that be only have records to reach.

Dear Kids

Dear kids, stay as young as you can,
It's really no fun being a grown woman or man!

We have bills, work, and we have to manage our time.
Everywhere we go, we have to wait in a line.

You know what's the worst? No more summer break!
And you can lose your job if you show up late.

Hanging with your friends, don't even think twice,
Everyone is busy, caught up in their life.

If you want kids of your own, you better hold on.
Your so-called workday is now twice as long.

So, stick to your homework and going to school,
Where the only thing you worry about is if you are cool.

And about that, just do it your way,
You're cool no matter what anybody else has to say.

So, go play outside and dance in the rain,
Read more books to work out your brain.

Laugh a lot more and always be a good friend,
Enjoy your free time because that will come to an end.

Listen to your parents when they try to instruct.
One day you might have a kid like you, and if so, good luck.

Don't think I don't like you, because that's not the case,
The day you were born, I saw an angel's face.

I'm just trying to teach you because sometimes you lose track
Of how good you have it, right now where you're at.

So just be a kid for as long as you can,
Growing up too fast should not be your plan!

I hope you take heed of all of these words,
But you probably won't, because teenagers are turds!

Just kidding (but not really).
Love, Dad!

Moms

We all know dads are tough, but when I started to read
About different types of moms, well, I just couldn't believe!

It's funny how male lions are King of the Beasts,
Yet the female lions are the ones who hunt for the feasts.

Take a black widow and how it can be,
The female with the red dot is the most poisonous, you see.

Then there's the praying mantis, I bet the males live in dread,
Once they make babies, females bite off their head!

You've heard about mama bears and how their baby is their heart,
If you get close to their baby, the mom will tear you apart.

Moms are so fierce, I have to say,
If they're ever upset, get out of their way!

If I get approached by a bully who's mean and strong,
Sorry Dad, but for my backup, I'm calling Mom!

The Race Car Driver

Once there was a boy named Rob who was sure he wanted to be a race car driver. He wanted to wear that big, beautiful helmet with the visor, those special driver clothes, and, of course, drive that magnificent car.

But his mom wasn't so sure. "Rob, if you want to be a race car driver you must be strong to keep turning that wheel at high speeds, durable to drive for a long distance at the fastest speed, and dedicated to the sport."

"Mom, I can do all of those things, and win races," said Rob, with a gleam in his eye.

Rob watched all the car races on TV and pretended there was a steering wheel in his hand. He leaned to the left as he turned it left and leaned to the right as he turned it right, just like the cars on the TV.

One day, his mom and dad took Rob to a car race where he could see all of the race car drivers and cars close up. Rob heard the roar of their engines as they began the race, and the wild cheering for the winner of the race at the end.

"Yes," said Rob, "that's what I want to do when I grow up."

"There's a place where you can drive go-karts around a track," said his dad. "It goes left and right, straight, and even through corkscrew turns. You would race against other drivers, which would give you a better idea about what it takes to be a race car driver. Would you like to go? I'll race with you too."

"Yes, yes, yes!" said Rob, too excited to even say anything but yes.

So off they went to the indoor race track, signed in, paid, and waited patiently for their turn. They bought two turns and each turn included going around the mile-long track 14 times in two races. They would race against 12 cars around the track.

"Oh boy, oh boy, I can't wait!" said Rob.

First, they received proper equipment; Rob got a red helmet and his dad got a blue one. After a short introduction about the car and what the different flags meant, they were shown to their cars.

Once they were in the cars, a special seat belt was strapped over their waists and over both shoulders. Then, with a push on the gas pedal, they were off.

Rob was so excited! He slammed his foot down, the go-kart roared to life. He zoomed right off! A right turn, a left turn, a corkscrew, then a long straightaway back to the start, and the first lap was done. Now on to the second!

Cars were passing Rob, but he was driving the best he could. Before long, a problem arose. All the quick turns, this way and that way, were beginning to make Rob sick. After 12 laps, he was definitely car sick, and at the end of the 14th and final lap, he was officially nauseated.

When Rob got out of the car, he unsteadily walked over to his dad.

"You okay?" asked his dad.

"Those quick turns really got me," said Rob. "I don't feel so great."

Rob's dad could see that his son was a bit green in the face, so he said, "Let's get a drink of water and sit down for a few minutes."

Twenty minutes later, Rob felt a bit better, and it was time for the next race. Rob put his helmet back on nervously and got back into the race car.

A minute later, they were off for the second 14-lap race.

This time, Rob was determined to not get sick. He turned left, he turned right, and went as fast as he could.

But it was to no avail. Rob started to feel really car sick and couldn't wait to finish his final lap.

After some more struggling, Rob finally made it over the finish line. He was sick and sweaty, and jumped out of the car as fast as he could. Then he sat down in the nearest chair, head spinning.

"Hey Dad," said Rob after he felt a teeny bit better. "I'm not sure that being a race car driver is for me anymore. Maybe I'll be an astronaut instead!"

Oh boy, thought his dad. "Sure son," he said. "But how about we wait to talk about that until you feel better. I have a feeling you're going to be in for a surprise."

About the Authors

Don Rose was inspired to write *When the Day Ends… and Dreams Begin…* because of his close relationship with his children and grandchildren. Don recognized the great talent of Javier Lopez, his son-in-law, when Javier penned a poem after the loss of Madison, the youngest child of Don and Jenny, in 2015. Together they wrote this book for all to enjoy.

Don is a graduate of the University of California, Berkeley, an Army veteran, landscape architect, artist, and on the Board of Papillon Center for Loss and Transition in Monterey, California. He lives in Carmel-by-the-Sea, California, with his wife, Jenny, and their dog, Uncle Frank.

Javier Lopez was born in Northeast Los Angeles. He is a Marine Corps veteran. While serving in the Marines, he had the chance to visit different parts of the country and got to live in Okinawa, Japan. His experience living with the Okinawans inspired him to learn more about other cultures. He has been writing poetry since the early age of thirteen. He loves getting lost in the words of his poetry, and especially loves seeing the smiles on the faces of those he shares his poems with. He is excited to share his poems and Don's stories with the world.

Javier currently lives in Brentwood, California, in the Bay Area. He is married to his lovely wife Holly, who is Don's daughter. Together, they have four beautiful children, Antonio, Sebastian, Chloe, and Giana, as well as their family dog Roxy, all who have helped inspire him to write these poems.

Reach the authors at roselopezbooks.com.

Index